No matter how hard he tries to help, What-a-Mess always seems to end up in trouble. As a punishment for all the chaos he has caused, What-a-Mess is not allowed to take his friends with him when he goes camping. But his friends turn up anyway, and What-a-Mess comes up with an ingenious plan to make sure that they all have plenty to eat.

From the ITV series produced by Bevanfield Films for Central Independent Television

Adapted for television by Tim Forder

Illustrations by Nigel Alexander, Primary Design

Licensed by Link Licensing

British Library Cataloguing in Publication Data
Muir, Frank, *1920-*
    What-a-mess goes camping.
    I. Title   II. Wright, Joseph
    823'.914[J]
    ISBN 0-7214-1311-0

First edition

Published by Ladybird Books Ltd Loughborough Leicestershire UK
Ladybird Books Inc Auburn Maine 04210 USA

Printed in England

FRANK MUIR'S
What-a-Mess Goes Camping

Based on Frank Muir's original concept and story, and Joseph Wright's illustrations

Ladybird Books

'Why are you wearing that silly thing on your head?' asked the puppy's beautiful Afghan hound mother as she gazed in despair at her scruffy son, christened Prince Amir of Kinjan but known to everybody, for obvious reasons, as What-a-Mess.

'It's my crown,' said the puppy, loftily. 'As a prince in an old Afghan royal family I am entitled to wear a crown.'

'But that's not a crown,' said his mother. 'It's a plastic colander. You stole it from the kitchen sink. And you should have emptied out the spinach before you put it on. Now take it back at once because the lady of the house is looking for it. And then wash the spinach out of your hair.'

'But it's my crown!' cried the puppy. *'Please* may I keep it? I'll only wear it on royal occasions, like being bathed or chasing the postman.'

The puppy's mother looked at the eager little face. 'No,' she said. 'Put the colander back, or you might spoil things. There is a special treat planned for the weekend. We're all going camping! At the seaside!'

'The seaside? Where I met my friend the Archbishop of Canterbury? Can I bring him and my other friends?' asked What-a-Mess.

'You can bring them all. You've been a good little puppy for such a long time now – *days* – that the family wants to give you a treat.'

What-a-Mess raced down the garden to tell his friends the good news. He called them by using his Special Emergency Call. He sat down on their tribal meeting place, an old sleeping bag in the shed, pointed his nose to the sky and bayed, *'Owwwwwwwweeee – everybody to Meeeeeeeeee...'*

They soon appeared. The Archbishop came galloping up, ears flapping at different speeds as he ran.

The cat-next-door appeared silently, as though she just happened to be there all the time.

Cynthia the hedgehog came twinkling through the grass at a surprising speed.

And Ryvita the ladybird flew delicately in and made a perfect landing on the tip of What-a-Mess's nose.

And when they heard the news! All invited to a camping weekend!

The family who lived in the house were equally excited. The man bought a super portable camping barbecue and tried it out on the patio.

What-a-Mess circled around, waiting for a chance to help. The charcoal glowed red.

The man loved to barbecue sausages – good old British 'bangers' that burst when they were nearly done.

'Time to put the bangers on to cook,' the man shouted as the family trailed back into the house to fetch the food.

What-a-Mess heard 'Time to put the bangers on to cook...' and sprang into action. Here was something he *could* help with. He went to the garage to fetch a box of bangers (left-over fireworks from bonfire night). Then he stood up on his hind legs and tilted the box so that about twenty Chinese Crackers cascaded into the hot embers.

The result was dramatic. The Crackers exploded in the barbecue, which fell over, and then they jumped about all over the lawn, spitting sparks and bangs.

The family ran out of the house. 'My new

barbecue!' cried the man. 'Who did this?'

Then he saw What-a-Mess crouching in terror under the garden seat, clutching the empty box of fireworks. The man was furious.

What-a-Mess was allowed to come camping
with them because they could not leave him
behind, but he was not to talk, or help, or do
anything but sit quietly the whole weekend.
And, as punishment, he was not allowed to
bring his friends.

Almost in tears, he called a meeting on the
sleeping bag and broke the bad news to them.

'Ho, ho!' said the Archbishop. 'That's the way
it goes. It would have been nice to have seen
that old beach where we first met, but it'll still
be there in a thousand years. There'll be
another time.'

'I've never seen a beach,' said Cynthia the hedgehog. 'Or the sea, come to that. But the sea probably doesn't do all that much. Just makes waves, and goes up and down and ...' She wasn't able to hide her disappointment so she shut up.

The cat-next-door showed no signs of emotion at all. 'You can meet a very common kind of animal at the seaside,' she said, flicking a whisker clean with a perfectly manicured paw.

Ryvita the ladybird said, '   ' but her voice was so tiny that nobody heard what she said.

So off the family went on their weekend camping holiday with What-a-Mess crouching silently and miserably in the back of the car.

When they got there, the man found a good spot on top of the cliff and put up a huge, round bell tent.

What-a-Mess was not allowed to help, even when everybody had to give a hand to put up the big centre pole.

The man erected his bent barbecue near the tent and started cooking much too much food. The heat control had been damaged when What-a-Mess had blown up the barbecue, so the man was overcooking all the food.

What-a-Mess hovered, hoping to help so that the man would forgive him and drive back home to pick up What-a-Mess's friends, who so desperately wanted to come on the holiday.

'More fuel for the fire!' shouted the man.

'Coming!' shouted What-a-Mess, seizing his chance.

He rushed into the tent where he knew there was a big pole sticking up, grabbed the pole between his jaws and pulled. The whole tent gave a sigh and the canvas collapsed to the ground about the puppy's ears.

An hour passed. Darkness fell. The man, with the greatest difficulty, had put the tent back up again. He went to the car boot and took out the old sleeping bag that had been in the shed. 'You sleep in this,' he said to What-a-Mess, quite calmly but with a vein twitching in his forehead.

'Do not come into the tent under any circumstances. You sleep under the stars. Is that understood?'

All alone in the darkness, on a strange cliff top, What-a-Mess sadly unrolled the old sleeping bag.

'Ho, ho! And about time, too!' said a familiar cheery voice. And there, in a fold of the sleeping bag, lay the Archbishop of Canterbury.

What-a-Mess unrolled more sleeping bag. The cat-next-door emerged next, tidying herself busily.

Finally, Cynthia the hedgehog appeared, fast asleep, with Ryvita the ladybird sheltering between Cynthia's prickles.

All What-a-Mess's friends were there with him after all.

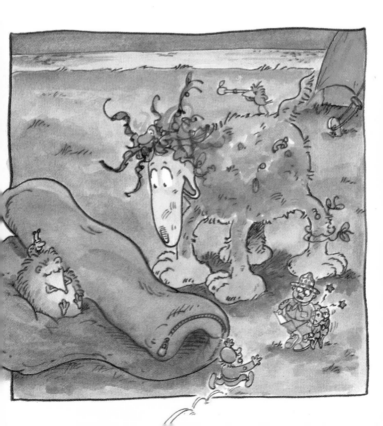

'It was that man in your house,' said the Archbishop. 'We were all having a snooze in the sleeping bag when he suddenly rolled us up and popped the sleeping bag into the boot of the car. We've been here hours.'

As the little animals awoke and realised that they were all on holiday with What-a-Mess after all, the puppy heard a strange rumbling sound. It was made up of a number of rumbles and could have been, the puppy thought, smugglers rolling little barrels of brandy up a pebbly beach.

'It's their tummies rumbling,' said the cat-next-door. 'They haven't eaten all day. Neither have I for that matter.'

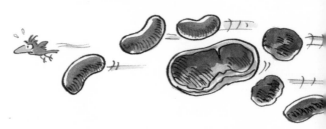

What-a-Mess thought. Suddenly he had the quickest good idea of his short, fat life. He raced down the cliff to the sea, rolled over in the water until he was sopping wet, and ran back up and into the tent to where the family was sitting.

'Let's all go swimming!' he barked, 'The water's wonderful!'

And he shook himself vigorously.

Ice-cold seawater flew off him and drenched the family. 'Get out!' they shouted. 'OUT! OUT!' And to make him go they threw at him the remains of their overcooked, much-too-much supper.

Outside the tent, the puppy's four friends, who were quietly rumbling on the sleeping bag, were suddenly aware that the air was full of flying food. Steaks, chops, bangers and pieces of cod were miraculously speeding through the flap of the tent and landing in front of them.

Hours later when the puppy and his friends
had eaten themselves to a standstill, they lay
down under the stars feeling very happy
indeed. When What-a-Mess had snuggled down
to sleep, Cynthia and Ryvita disappeared over
the edge of the cliff.

They reappeared a little later dragging
something behind them.

It was a child's rubber ring, which Cynthia and Ryvita had decorated with seaweed and coloured pebbles. They put it on What-a-Mess's head.

'It's a crown,' said Cynthia. 'Not much of one, I'm afraid. It's to thank you for our lovely holiday. Isn't it, Ryvita?'

'   ' said Ryvita.

What-a-Mess did not hear Ryvita because her voice was too tiny but what the little ladybird actually said was, 'Goodnight, sweet Prince.'

And at long last with his very own crown, Prince Amir of Kinjan fell happily to sleep.